The
Christ
of
Fish

The
Christ
of
Fish

YOEL HOFFMANN

Translated by Eddie Levenston

A NEW DIRECTIONS BOOK

The Christ of Fish is published by arrangement with the Harris/Elon
Agency, the Keter Publishing Company of Israel, and Professor Eddie
Levenston.

The Christ of Fish originally appeared in English translation in Conjunctions
24: Critical Mass in 1995, which marked Yoel Hoffmann's first publication
in the United States.

Design by Semadar Megged
First published clothbound in 1998
Manufactured in the United States of America.
New Directions Books are printed on acid-free paper.
Published simultaneously in Canada by Penguin Books Canada Limited.

Library of Congress Cataloging-in-Publication Data:

Hoffmann, Yoel.
   [Kristus shel dagim. English]
   The Christ of fish / Yoel Hoffmann ; translated by Eddie Levenston.
      p.   cm.
   ISBN 0-8112-1419-2 (alk. paper)
   I. Levenston, Edward A.   II. Title.
PJ5054.HG319K7513   1999   99-30395
892.4'36—dc21   CIP

New Directions Books are published for James Laughlin
by New Directions Publishing Corporation
80 Eighth Avenue, New York 10011

כריסטוס

The
Christ
of
Fish

שׁ

דגי

1

Two or three months before she died, my Aunt Magda remembered Wildegans's poem "Das Lächeln" and burst into tears. "I'm not crying," she said, "because Wildegans is dead, but because of the miracle that occurred when the funeral procession was held up by a traffic jam, outside our house in Vienna, for a whole hour." In an encyclopedia I found that the Austrian poet Anton Wildegans was born in 1881 and died in 1932, on the third of May.

2

So many things happened then, I thought to myself, just exactly the way they did (for example: burly bartenders, steins between their fingers,

"The Smile" (German)

were watching through the windows of the taverns). After all, Anton Wildegans died where Anton Wildegans died. You can't change his death to a pseudo-death.

When my father died ("I'm so . . . ," he said, and sank into unconsciousness) it seemed at first as though I still had my Father, but my father was a Dead Father. Among the books in his room, I found an old copy of Willson's English textbook. In Lesson Ten, on page sixteen, there were two oil stains (or egg stains) and against the word *dull* my father had written with a fountain pen *"nicht klar."*

3

Sometimes I dream that I am making love to a transparent seamstress (you can see her tailor's dummy through

"Not clear" (German)

LESSON X.
At Play.

The boys have come out to see the men at work. Four of the boys sit on the ground, and two of them play at see-saw.

One boy is up, and the other boy is down. Do you see the boy who is up hold up both of his hands'? Do you think he will fall'?

Do you see any tools of the men near the boys'? Do you know what tools they are'? One is an ax, and the other is a saw.

When boys go where men are at work, they should not touch the tools. They might get hurt, or they might dull the tools.

Do you see those little black specks up in the

her body) or that one foot is bigger than the other. When I read, for instance, that bamboo trees in the tropics grow a hundred or a hundred and twenty centimeters a day in the rainy season, in my mind's eye I see people standing among the green trunks (umbrellas in their hands), watching the trees rise slowly out of the ground. I imagine all kinds of things (like a man going into a stationery shop, asking for an exercise book with the lines close together, and dropping dead).

4

In Grade Three (a year after my father died) I wrote a composition:

What I saw in the market

I saw a mongoloid man in a fish shop. Every morning someone

combs his hair and dresses him in a white shirt. Afterwards they take him by the hand (maybe they say "Mr. Sun is in the sky") and lead him to the fish shop and there, in the shop, he stands all day by the tank and looks at the fish. How lucky he was to be born to the wife of a fishmonger!

At the bottom of the page the teacher wrote: You should have written *everything* you can see.

5

The first photograph of me is of a baby in a wooden tub. The baby is leaning with his elbows on the edge of the tub and looking (with furrowed brow) in the direction, forty years ago, of the camera lens. Later, in another photograph, the baby is sitting in a wooden high chair (wearing a gray pullover on which someone has embroidered NATAN) holding a metal toy in his two tiny hands. I no longer remember the baby, but I remember the toy (part of some utensil, maybe a kettle).

6

She was stubbornly sentimental, my Aunt Magda, about Anton Wildegans, the way she was about everything else. At the beginning of the fifties (Food was scarce in those days. Once a month, in exchange for government stamps, we ate a yellow chicken.) on Passover Eve, Aunt Magda's friend Berthe came to visit her and brought her from the Jordan Valley a large carp in a metal bucket.

Though there was a heat wave that day, and Berthe had traveled by bus to Afula and from there to Tel Aviv in another bus, there were still signs of life in the carp. Aunt Magda filled the bath with water and put the carp in it. Two whole days the carp swam up and down the length of the bath. On the third day Aunt Magda declared that the carp "thinks just like we do" and sent Uncle Herbert (an expert in Sanskrit) "to put the fish back in the sea."

Not long after, on Aunt Magda's birthday, Uncle Herbert went to a flower shop and brought Aunt Magda a bunch of jasmine. Aunt Magda felt the petals between finger and thumb and dumped the flowers on the table. "Since you're a scholar," she said, "you should know that flowers aren't made of plastic, they're made of flowers." At that time Uncle Herbert still

had his own body, but inside it was
eaten up with cancer.

7

Why am I telling all this? Because as I
go on telling the story, one day I'll find
out (inadvertently) what is the most
beautiful thing in the world. And
when I do, I shall say (even if it's a jar
of black pepper): "This thing . . .
this jar here . . . is the most beautiful
thing in the world."

8

I think about trifles, like the proper
way to count birds. It's hard to count
birds when they're flying about, so it's
better they should be at rest. They can
move their feet or flap their wings, but

if they're hopping from branch to branch or changing places, it's very hard to know how many there are.

9

Recently it has occurred to me that the world, despite what many people say, is properly set up. The things you find on the left (since there's no other, more apt name, let's call them "lefties") have a special quality which, if a man is gifted with the appropriate sense, will enable him to distinguish them from the things you find on the right.

10

My mother gave birth to me and died (in this sequence of events there is evi-

dence of perfect order) so my father
searched the books until he found me a
name you can pronounce backwards,
and remained (Dr. Theodor Weiss,
Ear Nose and Throat) alone.

11

I want to buy a sun and eat it. I'll leave
the shop and people will say: "Look!
He's rolling a whole sun along the
road!" They will all move aside. The
light will be awesome. At night the
sun will shine in my abdominal cavity
and light up Tel Aviv (and Zimmermann will say, "*Ick hob gesehen mit
mayne eygene oygen az er hot ir
afshtiker tsushniten un afgefressen*"
maybe twenty times).

"*With my own eyes I saw him cut it into pieces
and bolt it down*" (*Yiddish*)

12

It's not nice to tell so many stories about dreams, I know (you can say it all in one word but this word will be so terrible that the paper will catch fire). I dream that I'm roaming the streets of Kathmandu, or somewhere else, and asking: "Who is Sill?" I'm unmarried, that's why I'm asking. In the end, when someone declares that the touchstone (or the "philosopher's stone") is lost, I meet Sill (her face is full of pimples) under some iron steps.

13

When I think about death I imagine some large crooked Lithuanian saying "Oiss," or something exploding (like a donkey's spittle) and seeds being scattered. How many times can a heart beat, a heart of flesh and blood? There are so many things (nice and not nice) which get mixed up as the years go by. If it were not for my late Uncle Herbert (who taught me words in Sanskrit and did my arithmetic homework for me) I would be sure that it's impossible to know anything in this world.

14

Sometimes things happen which are quite unreasonable, like for instance German prisoners of war chasing butterflies in Shanghai. Someone (a retired mining engineer) is sipping tea. Is he standing? He isn't standing. His feet are bare (veins, etc.). The larynx in his throat goes up and down (two or three times). When you think that even in August this old man has a name of his own, your heart breaks.

15

Uncle Herbert died and six months later my father died. For seven days he gazed (with his eyes shut) on the events of his life. Afterwards, when his urinary tract was blocked, he spoke of Venice. The day he died, at quarter past eight, Shraga Wallach, the vice-principal, came in (I was then in Grade Two and every morning sang "Adon Olam—Lord of the World, who reigned before Creation") and said: "It's time for Weiss to go home."

16

I want to know how (by virtue of what principle) the universe keeps going. That is, why things don't suddenly vanish. Wherever (e.g., in railway stations and large hotels) there is an information desk, I want to ask, but I don't. But I swear one day after my father died, Aunt Magda stood in the kitchen and split a large block of ice with a hammer and screwdriver. The first one to leave her was her husband, Herbert. Then her brother, Theodor, my father. Yet the old turkey's passion for all kinds of things showed no signs of fading.

17

I remember how the almond tree blossomed in Palestine. My father held me (in the Arctic cold. I was a little penguin.) close to his belly and talked with Uncle Herbert, in the fields east of Ramat Gan, about Schopenhauer and Kant. A north wind was blowing. The air was very low. But I knew that if my father dropped me, Uncle Herbert (the big, childless penguin) would gather me up between his feet.

18

I want to know: what is the ontological status of the memory of smells? I picture in my imagination a Kirghiz philosopher (i.e., a philosopher who lives in that part of the world called Kirghizia and reads the *Critique of Pure Reason*) and when I hear the tune of "September Song"—Oh it's a long, long time from May to December—I cry.

19

There's nothing emptier than memories of childhood. Where is Herr Floimenbaum, who used to retrieve burnt-out valves from the wooden cabinets of radios? Where is the I who said to myself, "Can a plum tree mend electrical equipment?" and where are *they* now, the burnt-out valves?

20

When you write with a sharp-pointed pencil, you get a lovely, fine line. Aunt Magda, who was left by herself (i.e., she was left only with me), wore purple, had large rings, and became Pawel's lady friend. And since Pawel (an accountant) believed in the principles of the Baha'i faith, Aunt Magda traveled to Haifa, to the temple with the golden dome.

In those years (her purple years) Aunt Magda composed about twenty poems. And though she wrote most of them under Pawel's inspiration (in praise of the Baha Ullah, and so on) she

worked in a few lines (like "the hills
pass through my body, hill after hill"
or "sometimes I forget how great are
the heavens. I want to see the whole
firmament."), which would have flab-
bergasted Anton Wildegans himself.

Was Pawel Aunt Magda's lover?
Though she stood in the Persian Gar-
den between the rows of flowers with a
purple sunshade in her hand, it was
difficult to imagine Aunt Magda (who
referred to boats as "she" and called a
frog a "Frosch") in the act of love.
Aunt Magda had plenty of organs in
those days, but they all had another
clear and definite purpose.

21

I sink into deep sleep and touch the
fringe of death. I wonder: how far
down did Uncle Herbert and my fa-

ther go? They seem to me to be hover-
ing in the upper air of that kingdom
(beneath the glass plate) and looking
for me. The suits they brought from
Europe are no longer in fashion. They
are dead-old-men. They pass over me.
I shout, but they do not hear.

I ponder: "Socks and the brain are
precious things. When a sock gets
parted from its fellow sock, it also gets
parted from the brain. But the brain
draws near the sock and leaves the fellow sock behind a little. Afterwards
the fellow sock draws near the brain,
and the first sock gets left behind (*und
so weiter*). You have to take care that
one sock doesn't get separated from its
fellow by more than a pace, and that
they both stray away from the brain
by no more than the measure of the
body."

and so on (German)

22

In the empty space of the house there is now an old stethoscope (my father's ears are already transparent) and in the hallway, next to the overcoats, which date from the forties, two sick ghosts are sitting side by side. A pale copy (almost invisible) of Uncle Herbert is turning the pages of a German-Sanskrit dictionary, and Aunt Magda, blue as the eye of a flame, in the springtime sleep of the afternoon, wears on her face, for a moment, the expression of a child.

23

It is hard to imagine a god who snores, and even harder to imagine a great god who snores and a number of little gods who find it difficult to sleep. Someone says (Zimmermann or someone or other): "For vun hundred I buy fifty." A—he was born. B—he grew up (all those years). C—he was loved. D—he was fed and washed. E—they cried. F—all around him grew old and died and now he says "for vun hundred I buy fifty."

24

It must be May outside. Between the pages of *Everything You Wanted to Know, from A to Z* (published by Tcherikover, 1941), above a map of Burgundy, next to a profile of Buxtehude, there are butterflies flying. Zimmermann must drink nectar from calycine flowers and skim across the ocean with white seagulls. One white seagull, supremely beautiful, turns to Zimmermann and says, "My name is Jonathan," and Zimmermann says, "My name is Zimmermann."

25

Although my uncle, Herbert Hirsch, played the harpsichord, the ship on which he sailed for Palestine ran aground. The captain, leaning his chin on the back of his hand (like *The Thinker* by Rodin or sad women called Liliane), gave orders for eight large wooden crates and thirty horses to be thrown overboard. First the horses galloped (as if they were holy horses) towards the hills of Rhodes. Then they sank, horse after horse, and turned into little sea horses, transparent as glass.

26

The ship lifted off and floated, and my Uncle Herbert stood on the upper deck, his fingers moving of their own accord, as the air moved with the ship around my Uncle Herbert, who stood on the upper deck, his fingers moving of their own accord in the air around the ship.

27

My Uncle Herbert was a fat mystic (when he played on his harpsichord jackals and wild dogs howled. He made the glowworms dance.). But he didn't leave behind even one explicit sentence. Of the philosophic essay he was writing (he had given it the title "If the world changes—what will become of the laws?") there survived only the first twelve words: "Let us imagine a slice of sausage lying on the white keys. . . ."

28

Uncle Herbert, as Aunt Magda used to say, had "two left hands" and sometimes, I remember (when his hairy left hands were still part of his body), he cried in his sleep. Once he said: "One thing I know with absolute certainty." But he never said what it was. I was a child at the time, so what I'm about to say is likely to sound pretentious, but I'm ready to swear that Uncle Herbert (the fat gold watch) thought that the world both existed and didn't exist, simultaneously and indistinguishably.

29

In Palestine, at all events, he wrote a philological essay, and took an imaginary dog for a walk (Aunt Magda couldn't stand strong smells) along the dirt paths between the orchards. When the English (who were looking for terrorists) arrested him, he explained that he had left the house to escape from the heat and said (were the words translated from the Sanskrit?), "the personality ignores the oppressive heat within the shrine."

30

I dream that North Korea has put a man on the moon. Why has North Korea put a man on the moon? At first he jumps around like a kangaroo among the white rocks. All the air is inside his suit. His face and the world are divided by a Masonite screen. He longs for North Korean dishes. He lifts his gaze to the moon but the black skies are empty.

I wake up and dream again. The Norwegian King Hakon VII is cruising along in a taxi. Hakon VII tries to slam the door. But this controlled movement becomes involuntary, compounded of wind and momentum. For an instant you can see Hakon VII, door in hand, horizontally leaving the taxi. But a moment later (as when the head first breaches at birth) he is sucked back in.

31

My Uncle Herbert died and my father died and Berthe, who got away from Adolf Hitler in time and went to live in the Jordan Valley, fled from there on account of her husband, Adolf Hertz, and came to Tel Aviv, to Aunt Magda, crying and carpless. Aunt Magda, I remember, wrote to Berthe's husband and Berthe went out onto the verandah and came in and went out again and beat the carpets until a letter of reply came from Adolf Hertz and Berthe went back to the Jordan Valley.

32

Then came the days of Pawel. I sometimes wonder: if Berthe had stayed longer in Tel Aviv and met Pawel, would she have gone back to Adolf Hertz, to the Jordan Valley? One way or another, when Pawel appeared Aunt Magda was already on her own and Pawel, I think, heard about Berthe only from rumors.

33

Aunt Magda took over the expression "my late husband" and divided her life into two periods: "When my late husband was still alive" and "now." Sometimes, when she said, "Herbert used to say," tears would well up in her eyes. But if some omnipotent being had proposed turning back the wheel of time and restoring her late husband Herbert to life, she would, I think, have had reservations. Suddenly all the space between the walls of the house was hers. She put the harpsichord in the "guest-room" and over the old couch she spread a purple woolen blanket.

34

She turned into a kind of legendary bird. An albatross. Like a Sumo wrestler she thrust back alien authorities, and with the help of ancient strategies taught herself to say the right things. "First," she said, "my husband died of cancer of the liver. Six months later my brother, Doctor Theodor Weiss, passed away from complications following pneumonia." Her thoughts circled the periphery, like great ships.

35

She had a special recipe for apple cake and a glass mouse and an alarm clock that played a Viennese waltz at the appointed time, and she had a cherry-wood jewel box and an inlaid ivory salt cellar and a picture of a wagon done in embroidery and she had china dolls (a shepherd and a baby and some Italian noblemen) and silverware and colored postcards. And she had flowerpots.

36

I dream that the King of Norway,
Hakon VII, comes to Palestine, the
land of Israel. A warm wind is blowing. Someone shades the royal head
with a parasol. The King lifts his blue
eyes to the hills and someone hastens
to tell him that the burning shapes in
the east are called, in the ancient lan-
guage, "hills." They tell him that the
sea is called "sea" and the sky "sky."
But no one ventures to tell him, the
King of Norway, that flowerpots are
called "flowerpots."

37

I want to know: are there colors and
smells in the brain? The pig farmer is
dead and now the old sow is running
through the streets of my mind (across

wooden bridges) looking for him. And maybe the sights I see when I'm awake are someone else's dream?

38

Pawel was, in his own words, "an idealist" and though he owned two offices (one in Tel Aviv and one in Petach Tikvah), "a man," he said, "should strive for something else, more spiritual." Once, he said, he was a "confirmed follower of Spinoza" but now (i.e., then) he was closer to the position of the philosopher Moses Mendelssohn and like him (i.e., like Moses Mendelssohn) he was of the opinion that a man should adopt a rational religion, like the Baha'i faith, for instance.

39

They pierced his feet, the Son of God,
with nails, I know. There are some
things which it were better had they
not occurred. But if Pawel had been
there (i.e., in place of the Messiah) and
they had pierced *his* feet, I'm sure the
talcum powder he sprinkled so carefully between his toes (and the white
socks he changed every day after his
bath) would have shown everybody
that a man could, in spite of the filth in
Palestine and his bodily sweat, protect
himself against epidermal eczema.

40

Above all he argued for the eternity of
the soul. The scientific proof of eter-
nalism, he said, was the glowing aura

that could be seen round all kinds of things. He relied, I remember, on an aristocratic woman named Blavatsky, who had dipped her body in the Ganges and said a prayer for plants. The aura of a leaf, Madame Blavatsky said (Pawel said), remained whole even after the leaf was torn to shreds.

41

I want to know: what was Pawel's exact place (at seven o'clock on a Saturday morning when he went down to the sea at the end of Rechov Gordon with a straw hat and the *Reader's Digest*) in the vast order of the universe?

42

I immerse myself in the bath and see my father's body in the water. A thin man. A white soundbox. A slender violin for the reform of the world. A doctor for the vocal chords. . . did he hear the beating of birds' wings in the woods of Moldavia? Had he seen, in some old medical textbook, a picture of the inner ear?

I think about what sights are seen by the dead. At first the flesh relaxes. Then, in the vast silence, the great body of thoughts slowly, slowly, melts away. I try to picture in my mind total nullity. Non-existence. Nothing whatever. But I cannot.

43

When Berthe died, her husband, Adolf Hertz, came to Tel Aviv to pay Aunt Magda (this was in 1965) a "condolence visit." He sat, I remember, next to the harpsichord, in summer, wearing a black suit. "Just imagine, Frau Hirsch," he said, "to this very day I am still eating the cucumbers (he said *Gurken*) that my late wife pickled."

44

I think of the horse harnessed to the carriage that carried Claire Bloom and Charlie Chaplin in Hollywood, in 1950. The horse is dead. But it has acquired an aura (in the opposite direction to the arrow of time) and now, over and over again, times without number, harnessed to a two-dimensional carriage, it carries the dancer Terry to Clavero, the old comedian, in the London of 1910.

45

My father, Theodor Weiss, ear, nose
and throat specialist, said, I remember, "sinusitis" or "tympanitis," as
though man was nothing but a body of
flesh, though also an astral body with
an aura. And since he could see (by
virtue of the laws he knew) what was
destined to happen to it, to this body,
his heart was filled with great Hungar-
ian sorrow.

46

I remember how he walked the streets
of Tel Aviv and I walked by his side. It
was August or September, not long
after Uncle Herbert died and not long
before his own death. On the radio
Bing Crosby was singing "Autumn in
New York." On the old calendar

horses were galloping. Suddenly, I remember, I saw (in a prophetic vision)
my father, Theodor Weiss, born in
Budapest, crumple and fall and turn
into stars.

47

I love Vashti, and Cinderella's ugly sis-
ters (they stroke each other's lower
bellies. Their huge feet are fine for
acts of depravity.). And Jezebel. And
Rahab (the spies had already traveled a
distance of seven leagues from Jericho
when they turned on their tracks, went
back to the house of the Canaanite
harlot, and picked up the bunch of
grapes they had forgotten).

I love words like *Papagai* or *Tinte*.
A French aunt (Coquettish. Her body
gives off whiffs of cheap scent.) is
called *tante*. But a German aunt

(full-bodied) is called *Tante*. When a German aunt dusts the table and knocks over a bottle of ink, they say "*Schau* (i.e., "Look"), *Tante* spilt the *Tinte.*"

I'm very fond of Percival, of the conditional sentences. Percival in the sentence "If Percival had come" will never ever come (oh, dear!), but Percival in the sentence "If Percival came" even though he hasn't come, could still come (maybe). If Percival comes—to supper, for instance—I'll serve him cooked asparagus (with butter. Percival likes to dip his asparagus tips in butter.).

48

Percival was born in the county of Yorkshire to a family of fishermen. His father (through the bedroom window) cast huge fishhooks into the sea. When the other fishermen asked Percival's father why (through the bedroom window) he cast huge fishhooks into the sea, Percival's father told the other fishermen: "My father and his father before him cast (through this window) huge fishhooks and if my wife (he pointed to Percival's mother), by the grace of God, gives birth to male offspring, they too will cast (through this window) huge fishhooks."

When Percival was born the vicar rang the church bells. Everyone was happy. The fishermen's wives came to peek at the cradle (later Percival's father was to say "their heads stank of fish"). They killed a duck. They brought up an old bottle from the cellar and sang "My Bonnie Lies Over the Ocean" and "Sweet Lass of Richmond Hill."

During the third watch a crow cawed. The roofbeams creaked. Old Jeremiah (in his youth he had hunted whales in the North Sea) made the sign of the cross and said: "God grant I be proved wrong. But I fear (with a superstitious spit) nothing good will come of this child." Everyone crowded in the doorway. Southwest of Yorkshire there rose in the sky, lit by the light of the moon, a gigantic apparition, Philip Gross, my English teacher in Grade 5C.

49

. . . all the things that the heart forgets: seaweed, for instance, on the shore at Tel Aviv. Baklava. The Book of Nehemiah. Stomach juices. Inverted commas. Buckles. Cooking recipes. Flickering lights. Parcelation maps. Panes of glass. Bicycle tires. A drawing of an arrow and two hearts (or of two arrows and a heart) and names like "Kurt."

list

50

I picture in my mind a marine ornithologist. He is an expert on sea birds, and nevertheless one testicle has slipped into his abdominal cavity. People put up columns and inscribe on them "Here Napoleon repulsed the Turkish army" and so on, but no one would dream of erecting an obelisk to mark the place where a marine ornithologist pushed his testicle, with his own fingers, back into his scrotum.

51

First (I think) God created Matzliach Najar (with his white shirt and its horizontal black stripes) and only later (i.e., after he created our Arabic teacher) did he bring forth from chaos, slowly, in pain and wisdom, everything else.

How can you portray a man like that in words? Apparently (and actually) he was respected. People greeted him respectfully (they said, "Good morning, Mr. Najar"). And though he didn't know who Paul Hindemith was (and when people said "Lilliput" he thought they were laughing at him) his heart was moved somewhat when he heard on the radio, in Ramat Gan, the chorus from the Ninth Symphony.

I remember. Herzl, Benjamin Zeev, is leaning on an iron bridge and looking out to sea (He can see history, from beginning to end, in one gaze. "Everything," he thinks, "flows. You can never enter the same water twice.") to the right of the blackboard, next to the entrance. Our Arabic teacher's head stood free in the air. But his scrotum (everyone saw) was resting on the edge of the table like Isaac on the altar, in the story of the Sacrifice.

52

I remember Kaminer, who raked the body of Rabbi Akiva with iron combs. Blood flowed between the desks. Rabbi Akiva stood in front of the platform (his upper body naked) with prophecy on his face. "Parchment," he said (Kaminer shouted "Quiet"), "is burnt and letters blossom."

53

The vice-principal Shraga Wallach (his wife's name was Nordia) used to

walk the corridors, I remember, past
the hooks for the luncheon bags, looking for children. He was a communist.
"In summer," he said, "the windows
will remain open, even if everyone
wants them shut. In winter, even if
everyone wants them open, they will
remain shut."

When I think about Paradise I see
Shraga Wallach, his black hair cover-
ing the folds of his belly. He's the one
of whom Schiller sings:

> *Freude, schöner Gotterfunken*
> *Tochter aus Elysium,*
> *Wir betreten feuertrunken,*
> *Himmlische, dein Heiligtum!*

"In 1950," he explains to St. Peter,
"I left the Communist party and
joined, halfheartedly, Mapam."

> *O Joy, fair spark divine,*
> *Daughter of Elysium,*
> *We enter, drunk with fire,*
> *O heavenly one, thy shrine. (German)*

54

In Aunt Magda's room, on the eastern
wall, there was an old map of Budapest
(in summer flies and mosquitos used
to settle on the castles and churches of
Pest), and on the opposite wall there
was an oil painting of one Leopold
Weiss, Aunt Magda's great-grandfather, who was a confidential advisor.
A photographic portrait of Uncle Herbert (i.e., a picture of his body before
he died) stood between two plates of
glass on the harpsichord in the "guest-
room," next to the telephone.

55

When they brought it (i.e., the telephone) Aunt Magda became a butter-
fly. A spark of divine fire. Her ortho-

pedic shoes barely touched the floor. She covered it with a cloth (so that it shouldn't get dusty) and placed fruit in front of it and talked and talked into it (with reason and without), every day, to Pawel and to Frau Stier and to Doctor Staub, and many more.

56

She used to say: *"Die Pumpe ist zerbrochen"* and *"Mittwoch kann ich nicht"* and *"Also ich bin dort um zvei"* and "I want the Tax Department" and "My husband passed away two hours ago" and *"Stell dir vor"* and *"Stellen Sie sich vor"* and *"wunderbar"* and *"ausgezeichnet"* and *"leider"* and *"eigentlich."*

"The pump is broken," "On Wednesday I can't," "Well, I'll be there at two o'clock," "Imagine" (informal), *"Just imagine"* (formal), *"wonderful," "excellent," "unfortunately," "actually"* (German)

57

In Pawel's house, in those days, on Saturday nights at eight o'clock, conversations took place with the dead. And though the content of those conversations escapes me (did they ask after their health?), I know they spoke (with the aid of glass tumblers) with Madame Blavatsky and the Baha Ullah and Rabindranath Tagore.

58

Apart from Aunt Magda and Pawel, there took part in those meetings Herr Doktor Staub (who was a Doctor of Philosophy) and his wife, Hermine, and Frau Stier (who was the widow of a wine merchant) and, from Petach Tikvah, (the flesh of her thighs overlapped the seat of the bus) "Madame Edna," a clerk in Pawel's office.

59

Every Saturday afternoon at half past four (the air was already filled with the smell of coffee and apple strudel) Frau Stier would ring Aunt Magda's doorbell three times. And from the moment Frau Stier arrived (i.e., from half past four) until the two of them (i.e., Aunt Magda and Frau Stier) left, at 7:46, for Pawel's house, Frau Stier would talk to Aunt Magda and Aunt Magda would talk to Frau Stier.

60

I remember when Frau Stier said "*Wurzel*." That was a unique occasion. The wine merchant had died and his wife, by the grace of God, said "*Wurzel*." The roots of Frau Stier's teeth (apart perhaps from the one that had been extracted) were in her

"Root" German

mouth. There were roots in flowerpots. And at eye level, on the horizon,
spreading down into the earth's crust,
were hidden roots.

61

I picture in my mind the journey to
Haifa. A post-Mandate train. Pawel
in leather slippers. Aunt Magda's
Austro-Hungarian earlobe, like a purple cloud, passing through Binyamina
and Atlit. A Chevrolet taxi and the
heart fluttering at the sight of the
golden dome.

62

I can see the temple. Pilgrims from
Famagusta (nineteen of them. The
equivalent in gematria of "Wahad.")
are silently, their backs stooped, leav-

ing the office. Rising diagonally from Pawel's head, amid the scent of white-wash and roses, are beams of light with dust swirling around in them, as in some ancient painting.

63

They had dinner at The Cellar, on the corner of Allenby Street, where the head waiter was named Max. Pawel drew back Aunt Magda's chair and as she went to sit down pushed it under her body. On a metal tray Max brought potatoes and dead fowl.

64

Afterwards they took the bus to Ahuza and stayed with Frau Haupt from half past four till five forty-five or ten to six. This coffee hour on Rechov

Moriah, fortunately, took place after birth and before death. And though the Earth was revolving on its axis, the sea below the verandah did not overspill and the apple strudel was not overturned.

65

On the evening train they sat next to each other by the western window. Mount Carmel fell away behind Pawel's head. The reflection of the sun was doubled in the glass window. But Aunt Magda harnessed her body to the train and charged, like a dinosaur, through the fields of thistles back to Tel Aviv.

66

It was in those days, more or less, that Aunt Magda dealt in "stocks and shares." This matter involved Mr. Moskowitz, from whom Aunt Magda took advice (he was the missing hand at rummy) in Café Pilz. Mr. Moskowitz sat facing Jaffa. Frau Stier sat across the table from him, and Aunt Magda sat opposite Cyprus.

67

The cards they held in their hands cast their images in the sea. The crowns of the kings hit the Rock of Gibraltar. Off the coast of Libya queen mothers and jacks were reflected in the water. And between the isles of Greece, like gigantic octopuses, floated the bonnets of the jokers.

68

Sometimes, at high tide, sea level reached the ceiling of the café . Chocolate cake floated on the water. Aunt Magda and Frau Stier extracted pins from their hair and pinned the cups to the tablecloth. Their dresses billowed out between the wooden chairs like predatory flowers.

69

In '58, on Independence Day, Pawel fainted in the street. The force of life within him had dwindled greatly. First to leave his body were his thoughts. Afterwards, in among the petrol fumes of the tanks, he saw "Madame Edna," semitransparent, like an amber doll.

70

This inner vision put an end to the "Age of Pawel" in Aunt Magda's life and the "Age of Magda" in Pawel's life. When he came to, Pawel turned his gaze to an imaginary point and followed it from the corner where Rechov Frischman meets Rechov HaYarkon to Reading Power Station in North Tel Aviv.

71

What did Pawel see at the top of the chimney? Later he said (I believe him. You couldn't invent an expression like that.) that all the way there he was walking "on lots of swans." At all events, at the end of the summer Pawel married "Madame Edna" and Aunt Magda adopted the habit, Saturday nights as well, of frequenting Café Pilz.

72

In Café Pilz Mr. Moskowitz trod on his trouser cuffs. He looked like an old steamer. The cornfields of Romania grew from his nostrils. What did he do when he was alone? One can only guess. Perhaps (accompanied only by his brown horn-rimmed glasses) he took off his trousers and walked around on the cuffs.

73

 Sometimes the heart is fit to break. Such sanctity cannot be reckoned. How the skin enwraps the body. How the atmosphere surrounds the globe of Earth. And how, beyond the atmosphere, great bodies recede, soundlessly, into the gloom.

74

Any one of these people, single-handed (Frau Stier, for example, or Mr. Moskowitz), is capable of bringing the Redemption. Fire (radiant) is stored in their tissues. Their bones are phosphorescent. And their movements, like huge quasi-crabs, bring absolution.

75

When Pawel left her, Aunt Magda said, "I see that I can't see." Her eyes had weakened. She gazed upon imaginary flights of geese. But when the first rains fell (in the month following the New Year) she took a red umbrella and walked the whole length of Allenby Street, as far as the Opera House by the seashore.

76

Later, as pointed out, she got used to Pawel's non-presence. Yet perhaps her mind still fashioned scenes such as her coming to his house, placing on the table two jars with perforated tops and saying: "One is for pepper and one is for salt."

77

How the folds of her flesh moved from September into October! The sun rose and the sun set (a huge, blazing disc) and every day she carried around a brain called the encephalon. A woman beloved! Her smell was different from other people's.

78

In October (on the Eighth Day of Solemn Assembly, also known as the Rejoicing of the Law), Mr. Moskowitz clasped a scroll of parchment. He held the story of the Creation of the World tight against the nipples he had brought with him from Romania. Convex glass lenses separated his eyes from everything else. Did he rejoice in the law? Perhaps he remembered the picture he had seen from the window of the train: suddenly, between one hill and the next, sheep.

79

I want to ask: if these events were taking place in what they call a novel— would it be appropriate for Mr. Moskowitz to touch Aunt Magda's flesh? Should he touch Frau Stier's flesh? And perhaps (from some great hallucination) the three of them should let go of their cards and drop to the floor of the café, flesh upon flesh?

80

One way or another, the stocks and shares that Aunt Magda purchased (she called them *"papiere"*) yielded dividends, so she spread them, I remember, on top of the harpsichord, under the telephone. Frau Stier breathed in and breathed out. But when the rains stopped, her breathing subsided (what a wonder that there's a diaphragm!) into a kind of equilibrium, with the coffee and the apple strudel.

81

In April the sea blossomed. Scents rose from the water. The blue doors of gambling dens stood in the air. Christ lived. For in Café Pilz, in the afternoon, I remember, Mr. Moskowitz took a pinch of snuff from a golden snuffbox, and Aunt Magda trod the earth's crust as though she were a bird.

82

And the way the sun set. At about seven in the evening the great ball of fire touched down, and where it touched it stretched a little before it slowly sank, and though you couldn't see it from the café verandah, the salt water at that point must have boiled, for miles and miles. Afterwards, at the last moment before darkness was complete, there remained, as in a painting by Rembrandt, only the two hands of Frau Stier.

83

I want to tell you about Mr. Moskowitz. But what do I know about Jassy and Baku and Timişoara and Bucharest? A man should (through the power of logical analogy) be able to know everything. It should be possible, with the correct reasoning, to infer (from the present to the past) what Mr. Moskowitz, for instance, saw in Constantsa, in 1926, when he was a soldier in the Romanian army, through the window of the barracks room.

84

Maybe he remembers (he has no need of logical deduction) a widow named

Grigorescu and how (in bedroom slippers. Her ankles were exposed.) she
said, *"O domnu meu"* and no one could
tell whether she meant Mr. Moskowitz or God.

85

Many ships set sail from the port of
Constantsa. Some came back there
again and again. But no ship ever set
sail a second time on its first voyage.
How can ships break the time barrier?
The clocks show a different time and
the wood rots. Maybe one should spin
the great wheel on the bridge of the
ship simultaneously forwards and
backwards and then, in a flash, what
was will be again, for the first time
once more.

"Oh my lord" (Romanian)

86

In 1929 (actually on the eighth of May) Mr. Moskowitz came to Palestine, the Land of Israel. He was a young man at the time and the paraffin stove he saw in Jaffa took his fancy. He liked everything made of brass. But the white shoes he brought with him from Romania became covered with dust and the soles came apart from the soft leather of the uppers until there were gaping holes (where the toes were), like mouths.

87

In those days he certainly had dreams. A woman with a long neck kissed him (because he was "such a conservative") on the lips. His great-grandfather sewed him a book bag. But his dreams

were seen, as in a cinema, by him alone,
from within.

88

In 1930 Mr. Moskowitz (from cement
and gravel) built a breakwater. He
stood (like Prometheus when the ea-
gles plucked at his liver) with his face
pointing northwest, towards Constantsa, and his back to the monastery
on the port hilltop. *"Wer bin ich,"* he
thought (sardines slipped away between the rocks), *"ein anderer Moskowitz oder ich allein?"*

89

No doubt about it. The light was not
so sharp in the Carpathian Mountains.
Wild goats seemed almost to blend
with the blocks of granite and the furs

*"Who am I . . . another Moskowitz or just
me?" (German)*

of the foxes were of one shade with the pines. Why then be so pedantic about distinguishing between Mr. Moskowitz and everything else?

90

With Herr Doktor Staub and his wife, Hermina, Aunt Magda had already become acquainted in "the age of Pawel." Herr Doktor Staub was a disciple of Rudolf Carnap and therefore totally rejected "unscientific sentences." He came to the "conversations with the dead" on Saturday nights, so he said, only because of his wife who was, so he said, a decent woman though with strange interests.

91

Herr Doktor Staub divided the air into two segments. The right-hand segment was the air to the right of Herr Doktor Staub. The left-hand segment was to his left. In the middle, in the huge crevice, like a crow robbing the world of the transmundane, stood he (Herr Doktor Staub) himself.

92

I remember he said, "Ethics is *nicht absolutisch.*" He sat on the sofa and his wife, Hermina (a loaf of bread), sat next to him. At that point in time you could infer the covert from the overt in Herr Doktor Staub: pale buttocks, as though in anguish.

93

How the world played tricks on him. Birds deviated from the harmonies of Haydn. Field mice scampered with no reason. The sudden transformation from life to no life could not be properly explained by the philosophy of Rudolf Carnap. And Polish Jews garbled his name.

94

I remember (among the brighter visions) that I loved Hermina. She was—how can I put it?—a grassy lawn. A double bass. In all the surrounding bustle, she alone sailed the ship of Earth. And if something concrete must be said about Hermina—let it be said: on her right cheek she had a black mole.

95

I remember Mr. Moskowitz said, "*Ick shpazier zikh.*" His birth was a miracle, and there were other miracles that had

occurred since then. Hermina laughed.
But Herr Doktor Staub (perhaps the
use of a form denoting receipt of an ac-
tion rather than performance of an ac-
tion irritated him) clamped his jaws.

96

On the face of it, Hermina laughed
whenever occasions for laughter came
her way. Actually she laughed periodi-
cally (i.e., at regular intervals) and
things came her way, seemingly by
chance, whenever it was time for a
laugh.

I remember. Amalia Rodriguez
was singing on the radio. Children in
go-carts (as in a kitschy picture) were
sliding down the street. At that moment, as it were bisyllabically (first
"ho-ho" and then "ha-ha"), Hermina
laughed.

97

I would like to ask: how did Herr Doktor Staub come by Hermina? Did he
muster all his power of intellect and
mate with her (as with a hypothesis)
by force of utterance? Did Hermina
realize, as light breezes sported with
the folds of her dress, that this intellec-
tuality rose (like the skin on the top of
the milk) from *weltschmerz?*

98

Actually the story of Aunt Magda's
life is the story of Aunt Magda in her
corselet. Guns were fired at the *Alta-
lena.* Begin wept. But Aunt Magda
stood like a block of earth (such deci-
siveness is unparalleled), next to the
harpsichord, in her corselet.

99

She never thought (I think), "everybody dies. What's the point of those
elephant feet" . . . Hers was a different time. Rosier. And though she came
and went within the space between the
walls of the house, she said (when the
telephone rang), "Hirsch speaking," as
though names matched things.

100

I remember. She said, *"Ich bin ver-*
schnupft," and the word *"verschnupft"*
came right out of her nose. Not only
the chill but the word itself was in her
body. Her sense was common sense.
But her head stood in the window like
an oil painting of a Dutch Frau, and
out of doors, a cosmic corselet, crows
flew by.

"I've caught a cold" (German)

101

I would like to ask: Did my fat uncle, Herbert Hirsch, sit on the back of a donkey? He said *"Hops, mein Esel,"* and the donkey moved on, from category to category. Clouds of dust blossomed from his gallop. His hooves hardly touched the planet Earth. At one moment he was in a plane of observable time and space, at the next in a place where things are what they are, by virtue of their own selfhood.

mystical

102

The donkey's hide quivered with pleasure. There were beads of sweat on the tips of Uncle Herbert's hairs (on his chest). What was "agricultural unity" to him? What did he care about "Settlement Square"? The British may

"Let's go, my donkey" (German)

have had a mandate over Palestine, but
Uncle Herbert had a mandate over all
the worlds.

103

Like Leibnitz and like Hume he dis-
tinguished between factual truth (like
/"there are living creatures in the sea")
and tautological truth (like "all fish are
living creatures"). He disputed with
Kant. But, alas and alack, he did not
realize that the carp (*Cyprinus carpio*)
that Aunt Magda had bade him "put
back in the sea" was destined to die in
the salt water.

104

Oh, female carp! Could you see Uncle
Herbert from the water in the bucket?
Did you think: "There are duplicate

worlds but with a kind of isomorphy between them, for the carp in the other world is also swimming whither I swim"?

105

I remember. Uncle Herbert was clutching the carp in two hands as though it were a precious manuscript. His legs grew tall. His head was lost in the clouds. Then he let it fall, with the gentlest of movements, into other, sweeter waters among the stars.

106

In 1965 someone (perhaps his name was Alfred Windishgratz) snatched Aunt Magda's purse. Aunt Magda shouted "Schtop!" and ran down Rechov Reines. But at the point where

Rechov Spinoza begins, she stationed
herself under a street lamp and threw
out (as though in evidence that the
world was out of joint) her arms.

107

What did the thief do with her cards?
One can only surmise. Perhaps he
shuffled and dealt (himself) a hand of
patience in the Florentine quarter. At
all events, Aunt Magda bought herself
a new kidskin purse and gave instruc-
tions for the letters H dot M (in
Gothic script) to be inscribed on the
clasp.

108

In the summer of that year Berthe died
and Adolf Hertz came from the Jordan
Valley to pay Aunt Magda a "condo-

lence visit." Frau Stier was sitting on the old sofa. From Frau Stier's pelvic girdle stretched the bones of her legs (her pelvis and the two femora) but you couldn't see them for flesh and dress material.

109

It was very hot. Adolf Hertz spoke, you will recall, of the cucumbers "his late wife" had pickled. Suddenly Aunt Magda (perhaps Adolf Hertz's words had brought to mind some latent conjunction of events) said: "I remember how Bertschen and I ate corn on the cob next to the Opera House."

110

No doubt about it. Adolf Hertz had no desire to return to the Central Bus Station. Both of them, so he must have thought, were widows (perhaps he thought "each of them has a mouth like a vagina") but at ten to two he said (almost against his will): "Na . . ." and rose to his feet, and Aunt Magda rose to her feet, and Adolf Hertz didn't dare take it back and say, "What I said was just, as it were, a sigh."

111

I remember the maker of tombstones. In 1965 Simcha Bunis was already dead. But in 1954, when Aunt Magda asked what was the meaning of the letters *Peh Nun*, Simcha Bunis said (perhaps he thought to himself, "In a very little while I shall be strumming on transparent strings"), "Here lies," and his assistant Chmisa, like a distant echo, answered Amen.

112

Then Simcha Bunis spread an old newspaper on Uncle Herbert's tombstone and placed on it a loaf of bread, a hard-boiled egg and a cucumber. He may have crunched the cucumber (our memories play us tricks) and said, "You leef in Tel Aveef?" or he may have wrapped himself in silence. At any rate, at that moment the last angels urged him: "Simcha Bunis, take a wife!" *Magda*

113

What did Simcha Bunis see during his earthly life? Walls of clay? Huge blocks of stone? Gold dust? His body was made of cell upon cell (like the cells of monks) and tiny creatures moved within each cell. Simcha Bunis (this became clear only after his death) was made entirely of protoplasm, and within each cell of his body there was a membrane and a nucleus.

114

In the late sixties the flesh on Aunt Magda's arms became emaciated. Time carved lines on her face. In a kind of perpetuum mobile she re-~~*~~ *dehumanizes* volved around the three sides of a triangle whose apexes were her house, Café Pilz, and the house of Frau Stier.

115

She acquired a new trait, a kind of affectation: she would recite verses from the works of Anton Wildegans. She listened to records (Marlene Dietrich singing "Falling in Love Again") and when Frau Stier's turtle fainted from the heat (in August. On Memorial Day for the destruction of Hiroshima.) she said, "*Das arme Tier*" six or seven times.

116

She recolored all her memories: Herbert Hirsch was once again a young lecturer in the School for Languages. The Prater was covered with trees. Her dresses were bathed with color from the Danube and into the huge beer mugs were poured firkins of sun and stars.

117

In 1968 someone snatched the kidskin purse. The reader must be saying to himself: "In those days there wasn't so

"*The poor creature*" (German)

much purse-snatching in Tel Aviv."
Maybe not. Maybe only two purses
were snatched. But they both be-
longed to Aunt Magda (the one
snatched in Rechov Reines and the
one made from kidskin).

118

You may ask: what is the meaning of
purse-snatching? You may also ask:
what is the meaning of everything
else? Large objects determine the
movement of celestial bodies and this
movement determines the movement
of a purse.

negates
coincidence

119

I remember that my late uncle, Herbert Hirsch, looking from his window
saw a thousand birds. He may have

been seeking a word he had forgotten. He may have remembered the burning of the Zeppelin (at first the helium soundlessly caught fire. Then, as from a huge stomach, burning bodies and sheets of material tumbled out of the airship.). At all events, the birds migrated north. Not nine hundred and ninety-nine. Not a thousand and one. A thousand birds.

120

Did Aunt Magda give birth to a stillborn child? Did the baby float in her body (like the robbers who hid in the jars of oil), with eyes shut and skin soft as a frog's? And what would they have called the baby? Philip Emmanuel? Constantine?

121

The birds crossed the glass frontier.
My Uncle Herbert wiped the butter
from his mouth. He then read aloud
(perhaps from the *Bhagavadgita*) a list
of verbs—*pasjan, srinvan, sprisan,
svapan, svasan,* and so on—one after
the other, as if in prayer.

122

In 1969 Aunt Magda got to know
André, who was a philatelist. André
made use of French words (*"malgré
lui"* and *"sauerkraut avec sausages"*)
and when he talked about stamps (he
was a member of the Philatelic Association of Grenoble and assistant to the
Association of Jaffa–Tel Aviv) he
placed his fingers together and twid-
dled his thumbs.

123

In his jacket pocket André kept a magnifying glass the size of a saucer, and in his waistcoat, in brown envelopes, he hid stamps. On his desk stood Zumstein's catalogue, and Gibbons's and Michel's and next to Schnek's book (*Histoire du Timbre Poste*) there stood like a bookend, an iron box.

124

What was André concealing in the box? A postage stamp printed in Mauritius? A plaster cast of his lower jaw? At all events, in Café Pilz, above the hands of rummy, he gazed at Frau Stier and Aunt Magda as if they were rare stamps (with an error in the design or a printing fault).

125

André's first wife had taken her own life. Maybe she had a predisposition to suicide. Maybe she was just allergic to stamps. Anyway she made herself a preparation (with scrupulous care. The way you clean a baby's ears.) of potassium cyanide and strychnine.

126

First her neck grew rigid. Then her muscles twisted in opposite directions. The slightest noise sounded in her ears like the crash of thunder. Finally, as her diaphragm shrank and all the air passages were blocked, her eyes teared and she saw a large bubble, transparent as glass, in which were celestial landscapes.

127

I want to talk about eschatology (i.e.,
the study of last things). What will
happen in the days preceding the coming of the Messiah? First the Resurrec-
tion of the Dead. Parts of bodies which
got separated will come together (the
right arm and the right shoulder, etc.).
In full view, as in a field of corn, the
dead will straighten their upper bodies.
The moon will turn to blood. Stars will
deviate from their courses. Stones will
give voice. And then, at one stroke (as
at the death of St. Vitus who was
stricken with chorea) the primeval silence will be restored.

128

If André's second wife had thrown
herself off a multistoried building, you

could tell how she flew and flew. But André's second wife was a clerk in the office of a piano distributor, and every time someone struck the keys of a new piano, she would turn her face (like a mother pelican) towards the warehouse.

129

Maybe she thought to herself: "Examining a new piano again." And maybe she thought: "Something's going on in the warehouse." These two thoughts are not so very different. But since André's second wife didn't have too many thoughts, one should examine each one carefully and note even the slightest shade of meaning.

130

Did André's second wife stand behind his back like the fat woman in the painting *The Poet and the Muse?* She too (like the Muse) was wearing a cloak of sackcloth, with necklaces around her throat. She too (from arthritis) had her right arm stuck out. And though André was not holding a goose quill between his finger and thumb, in front of his feet too (as in the oil painting by Rousseau) ten roses bloomed.

131

It was about this time, more or less, that Aunt Magda, in her fur collar (between the hairs of the silver fox), found worms. They may have been "flatworms," no more than absorbent tissue, or they may have been "roundworms," whose nervous fibers (not anxious fibers. Nerve fibers.) ran the whole length of their body, as far as their sexual organs. At all events, she used the general term—*Wurme* (from the Latin *Vermes,* worms).

132

No doubt about it. She was very attached to her fur collar. But there was in those days a kind of gaiety about her that had no need of external objects. Her vitality derived directly from the life force within her. She listened to Antonín Dvořák's *New World Symphony* and sprayed herself with eau de cologne. When the telephone ran, she put the earpiece to her right ear and let the mouthpiece fall into her bosom, between the flesh and the edge of her corselet.

133

She was the sun around which the rest of the stars revolved. Frau Stier, like a satellite, presided over the innermost orbit. The other orbits were taken up by André and his second wife, Mr. Moskowitz, Herr Doktor Staub and his wife, Hermina, and Adolf Hertz, who came again from the Jordan Valley, carrying in his arms (the way you hold a baby) a glass bowl.

134

There was nothing risible about Adolf Hertz's proposal of marriage. First he placed the glass bowl on top of the harpsichord. Then he wiped the beads of sweat from his brow. Finally he said: "Seeing that you . . . that is to say, your late husband . . . and I

. . . that is to say, Berthe . . . I thought, I mean, the two of us . . . we should get married."

135

Aunt Magda was not as particular about the unnecessary use of name and number as Adolf Hertz. She seems to have foreseen the course of events. She skipped the preamble (she probably just said it to herself) and all she said to Adolf Hertz was: "We shouldn't be too hasty."

136

Adolf Hertz sat himself down on the chair in front of the harpsichord and the huge screw turned on its axis (from the inertial momentum of the body) a hundred or a hundred and twenty degrees. Thus with his face to the corner of the room (i.e., to the space between the two walls) Adolf Hertz cleared his throat and said: "She . . . that is to say, Berthe . . . used to put fruit in the bowl."

137

On the Day of Atonement a dead cock sailed through the air in centrifugal fashion, and at the end of the Concluding Service, when the *shofar* sounded, through the window on Rechov Bogroshov were revealed the ten Kabbalistic spheres. At the top, in transparent vapor, *'Ayin*—Nothingness—was concealed, and from it emanated, as in perpetual birth, the other nine. The Godhead, which had become divided, mated with itself face to face and back to face, and this act of creation was attended by Mr. Moskowitz (prayer shawl and all) backwards and forwards, in complete devotion.

138

What did Mr. Moskowitz see in the world of emanations? His great-grandfather Reb Mendel, who cut up a cow? Something sublime? A female maidenhead? At that moment, though, when the rams' horns sounded, his was a spiritual body and his sweat gave off a holy smell.

139

Afterwards, at home, he washed his horn-rimmed spectacles in water and took some fish cakes out of the refrigerator. Down in the yard a woman (it may have been Shoshanna Mirkin) shouted "*Vos art mir?*" and in the dome of heaven shone a hundred thousand . . . no. A million stars.

140

In the autumn Herr Doktor Staub went to Vienna. Doubtless he pictured himself meeting Moritz Schlick and sharing a fine meal with Hans Reichenbach, as in former days, in the restaurant near the museum. But Moritz Schlick died in 1936 (after rejecting the philosophy of Rudolf Carnap and Otto Neurath) and Hans Reichenbach died in 1955.

141

Did he (like Mr. Hyde. With tufts of hair in his ears.) cross the Seiler-

"What do I care?" (Yiddish)

strasse? Did he stand in the "Stepperl" emporium under a plethora of sausages? What is remembered from the journey is only that the heel of Hermina's shoe caught in the cobblestones, in Mariahilferstrasse, opposite the display window of a florist's.

142

First she removed her foot from the stationary shoe (as did her reflection in the window, among the gladioli). Her other shoe she dumped in the garbage bin. Then (like Lady Godiva, who rode her white horse naked through the streets of Coventry) she walked barefoot as far as Johann Strauss Street, the site of their hotel.

143

In 1970, in August or September, Aunt Magda and Frau Stier climbed to the summit of Mount Canaan (like ancient pilgrims to Canasta). Pinecones scattered coniferous seeds on their heads. Butterflies skimmed between their fingers. Frau Stier lifted a red heart towards the Sea of Galilee and Aunt Magda held black clover leaves.

144

That evening (in the lobby of the sanatorium) an elderly conjuror plucked handkerchiefs from his ears. Pigeons, dice and worry beads rose from his head. But when the clock chimed, he put the whole world (rabbits and teaspoons. Just like the Pied Piper of Hamelin.) into a suitcase.

145

The next day, when the sun was shining, Aunt Magda and Frau Stier looked at Beit Grossinger. Afterwards they both looked at a cow. And thus it was that, among the thistles, under the radiant light of the Land of Israel, Aunt Magda and Frau Stier stood still for almost a minute, as did the cow (and the cow in Aunt Magda's eyes, and the cow in Frau Stier's eyes, and Aunt Magda and Frau Stier in the cow's eyes).

146

No doubt about it. The cow knew nothing of the rules of Canasta. What would she have done with the four jokers? Something else attracted her attention: perhaps the orthopedic shoes or perhaps, under her piece of nylon netting, the blue tint that Frau Stier had applied to her hair.

147

On Friday Aunt Magda and Frau Stier came down from the mountain in the red Zeppelin of the Egged Bus Company. In Safed they had already placed their suitcases over their heads. In Meron, near the Holy Tomb, chickens were sucked into the airship, and at Majd el Krum the air was filled with the smells of hyssop and smoking charcoal.

148

Suddenly they saw the sea. It may have been there before they saw it, or it may have been created by the power of their gaze. At all events, sailboats were leaving the fishing port of Acre and making towards a large ship on the horizon, between Cyprus and the coast of Lebanon.

149

When André met his second wife he thought, *"Je me marierai"* (or *"Je me marierai avec elle"*). Why did he think in the reflexive? Did he imagine that the events destined to take place would be autokinetic (i.e., coming back upon themselves) like getting dressed?

150

Perhaps he remembered the brachial bones of his first wife or the sight of her swollen blood vessels. Maybe he was attracted by the extreme fineness

"I'll get married" (literally: I'll marry myself)—*"I'll marry her"* (literally: I'll marry myself with her) (*French*)

of the hairs all along her arm. But
memories, André thought, are but
fantasy. Nothing more.

151

He was not surprised that his second
wife was not dead. Her life, in her
sackcloth cloak, seemed to his eyes like
lotus petals drawn on a wall. He probably saw visions: her head lying on the
floor between two iron beds, and her
enormous feet free in the air.

152

Once he had climbed Mont Pelvoux,
whose summit reaches 3,954 meters.
Down below, like a fur collar, there
were woods. Above them, where the
air was thinner, were scattered patches
of *Calluna vulgaris* and all kinds of

mosses and lichens. But near the snow line there were expanses of meadow, where primroses, cinquefoil, and anemones bloomed.

153

André had never seen wolves, they were long extinct. And if there were a few left, they must have been hiding in the tundra, beyond the fields of flowers. Did André (in his youth, too, André was a philatelist) see that high above, among the glaciers, alpine butterflies were turning black?

154

I remember André and his second wife sitting on Aunt Magda's old sofa. André said, *"On s'habitue"* (i.e., "one gets used to it") and his second wife opened her mouth but never made a sound. The fat carp-lover was standing—like the tongue of a pair of scales—in his portrait photograph on the harpsichord, and behind him stood the glass bowl that Adolf Hertz had brought from the Jordan Valley.

155

In 1971 something went wrong with Aunt Magda's body. The fibers that extend along the atria of the heart did not contract properly, and the blood (corpuscles, thrombocytes, etc.) was compressed in her pulmonary artery and her aorta as though the chambers of her heart were occupied by drunken trombone players.

156

The family doctor (his name, I remember, was Doctor Mendelssohn) said: "With . . . tss tss . . . Frau Hirsch, a heart like yours you can live . . . tss tss . . . a long time." He then told Aunt Magda that his cocker spaniel bitch (tss tss) was still alive.

157

No doubt about it. The old dog's heart beat more strongly than expected. But her territory had been greatly reduced. Her memories (apart, perhaps, from the smells of a certain month of May) had dulled. Things seen in the room looked to the dog like a vision of creation: at first, chaos (bedsheets on the window sill) and waters cover the face of the floor. And when the dry land is revealed, the large pieces of furniture come back into place, and the air is pure and someone spreads carpets on the earth.

158

That year Aunt Magda looked at the moon as though through glasshouses. She wanted to visit London "just once." But her travel agency was situated in the middle of a melon field, and whenever she went to book a ticket, the clerks would disappear into a room and make love.

159

I remember she came to a halt six or seven paces before a death notice. The name of the deceased (above it were printed the names of all the cinemas)

had been pasted on a round obelisk, at
the intersection of Rechov Montefiore
and Rechov Nahlat Binyamin. Her orthopedic shoes stood side by side on
the pavement within the bounds of a
single stone without crossing the
cracks, as though she were playing
hopscotch.

160

That was quite an extraordinary moment. Cherubs (looking like naked
children) hovered near the verandahs.
Automobiles sailed by in silence.
Wholesale traders and barbers moved
their jaws beyond the shop windows,
and when she turned northward into
Allenby Street, all these sights moved
with her.

161

What were the roots of this great Aunt Magdalenian optimism? It was then, believe it or not, when the veins in her legs were turning blue, that she stood by the old water tower in Shavei-Zion and had her photograph taken. That was, I recall, a very merry journey. Frau Stier's hats sailed on the wind. Herr Doktor Staub said, "Yah, yah" and Hermina waved and every twenty miles or so, till the outskirts of Naharia, she laughed.

162

In the Penguin they drank iced coffee through glass straws, like the apostles of some Antichrist in a demonic version of *The Last Supper*. Afterwards they sat (all four of them. Herr Doktor

Staub and his wife, Hermina, and Aunt Magda and Frau Stier.) in a horse-drawn carriage. And either because of the refraction of sunlight, or for some other reason, it seemed the horses would not stop at the end of the avenue but go on, over the stone wall and across the beach, into the sea.

163

What did Mr. Moskowitz think when he saw Frau Stier for the first time? This is not to be spoken of, since Frau Stier is not a subject for discussion. But it certainly is possible to speak of Julia. When Mr. Moskowitz was four or five years old, his mother (Mrs. Moskowitz) baked cakes. And the cakes that Mrs. Moskowitz baked were sold, across the counter, by Julia.

Mr. Moskowitz could not remember whether or not Julia wore hats. But cake crumbs clung to her dresses and he did remember (he most certainly did!) how Julia knelt down in front of him and placed in his hand ("when you grow up you'll marry me and no one else") three transparent marbles.

Mr. Moskowitz grew up and Julia grew even further. She became as tall as a telegraph pole and the crumbs that clung to her dress turned hard as stone. He left the transparent marbles behind when he set sail for Palestine. But the vow he made was not annulled even on the Day of Atonement.

Did he imagine himself giving birth to the child that Julia should have borne? Did he see symbols in his sleep? Did he have a revelation (a real one; i.e., in the physical world) of a cloud of birds and a child, and the child is flying and he (i.e., Mr. Moskowitz) is left alone?

164

In 1972 Doctor Mendelssohn died. The old cocker spaniel doubtless wondered what had happened to the shadow of the man who wore the shadow of a hat. The human hand that stroked her spine gave her great pleasure. But she too was by now, almost entirely, antediluvian. The year Doctor Mendelssohn died was . . . how can one put it? The Year of the Dog.

dog is more alive

165

On the seventh day after the death of Doctor Mendelssohn, Aunt Magda said (in her bathroom. With nothing on.), "*Wo ist die Seife?*" The water reached the rim of the tub. Steam filled the room. And from the middle of the haze, like the mammoth that was found (fur and all) in Siberia, she asked for a piece of scented Yardley's soap.

166

What was she thinking as she washed her large body? Here are my arms? Here is the umbilicus, once attached by blood vessels to the belly of Eva Weiss? Here are my heels? Perhaps she sailed her balneal ship beneath the full moon and her flesh shone by the light of some other celestial body, even more distant, until you could see (as in some cosmic X-ray) the filigree pattern of nerves.

"*Where is the soap?*" (German)

167

I would like to know. Who loved Aunt Magda? Who did Aunt Magda love? Her loves began (in both cardiac directions) probably when she was still a baby. Her father, Isidore, covered her with a woollen blanket, and Eva Weiss (outside the window, like in a fairy story, piles of snow) tucked the blanket under the bed.

Isidore thought: I'll put my two feet under her tummy, and I'll set her flying and she'll scream. I'll bend my knees and she'll drop down. I'll roar like a lion and she'll grasp her toes, half in joy and half in terror, with her tiny little fingers.

Eva thought: How I love this little girl! I'll clothe her and feed her and tell her what little girls ought to know and when she cries I'll stroke her hair and

say "everything will be all right" or
"once I too was . . ." or "don't cry,
baby. Please don't cry."

And their visions of dread. Her
tiny body (this was Isidore's) slips out
of its diaper and continues to fall,
through the force of gravity. She falls
very slowly. And wonder of wonders!
Before she touches the ground (while
still in the air) you can see she has broken her skull.

And Eva. The birth. Her stomach
(her own. Eva's.) is splitting open from
the force of the thrust. Her face is
twisted. Her skin is torn. Only her
nipples are swollen, her inside is
empty, there is nothing in her but
breath (which goes round and round
and back again) and milk ducts.

168

In 1973 André sailed for France and his second wife, on a different ship, followed after. Her innermost thoughts were probably of pianos, legions of pianos. Her ankles hurt. When she stood on the deck her sackcloth gown flapped in the wind, and the huge raglan sleeves slapped her on the back and on the chest like elephant's ears, or large flags.

169

At Marseilles André stood on the quayside. When he had sailed for Palestine, ten years before, small engines were crossing the dock and his first wife (her voice choked with emotion) had said, *"N'est-ce pas? N'est-ce pas?"* He (André) didn't have any imagination. But that day, after the night journey through the Alps around Grenoble, the Greek ship seemed entirely covered (iron plates and funnels) with orange blossom.

170

Especially he remembered the heat of the sun. The heavenly furnace (from zenith to nadir) spewed forth rivers of fire. On the shoulders of the stevedores, in a mass of black hair, glittered diamonds. And as the ball of light finally set towards Malta, and the chalk cliffs of the Marseilles shore were swallowed up in darkness, the ship quietly moved off to the east and his (first) wife said *"enfin"* or *"on y va."*

171

That year Mr. Moskowitz asked his dream: Who was Moishe Zainder? Moishe Zainder, the dream replied, was the uncle of your mother, Rachel Zainder of blessed memory, and he died because of a swastika, or some other, simpler, cross. Go (said the dream) and find him, his form hardened, sitting as he was when they killed him, sidelocks and various accessories, at the corner of Popakitsu Street and Tranedafira Street.

Mr. Moskowitz didn't understand the dream's reply. But in his heart waxed a great love for Moishe Zainder and he pictured to himself the gesture (finger touching thumb) that Moishe Zainder used to make. Perhaps he saw shop signs written in Romanian, perhaps he saw cherubim. One way or the other, there's no doubt that he said "Listen . . ." or at least "Li . . ." and everyone thought that at the last moment he wanted to listen to a symphony of Anton Bruckner's or some Christian hymn.

How his soul marveled as it left the body! All those who stand around the dying man as the soul leaves the body are obliged to tear their garments, though the Germans and Romanians who stood round his body not only didn't tear their garments, they tugged at them to straighten the creases, like bloodstained dancers in the pause between one leap and the next.

All this and more Mr. Moskowitz saw in his sleep. Which is why he rose to his feet and made a huge tear in his nightshirt, and withdrew three fingers and tore it again, down to the bulging

flesh on his arm, across to his heart, as
though first his father and then his
mother had died.

172

On the Day of Atonement (there was a
war on, I remember) the harpsichord
sounded. Did the strings vibrate
by themselves? Did ghosts fan the
mechanism? Herbert Hirsch rose out
of the glass bowl, bearing on his chest
(like a large diamond reflecting the
rays of the sun) the body of a carp.

173

What did this hologram want in the
world? Magda, my arthritic aunt?
An old manuscript? Perhaps he was
doomed, my Uncle Herbert, by some
strange karma, to come back from the

realms of the dead (like a Christ of fish) in times of woe?

174

I remember the bottle that Pawel brought to Aunt Magda in the mid-fifties. The other memories are nothing but a reflex of things that were and are no more. But from the memory of that bottle there rises to this day an odor of woman's underclothes.

175

Did peasants' wives wipe their fundaments on vats of wine? Did they squeeze the wooden stopcocks (as in the relic of some Dionysian rite) between their buttocks? At any event, Pawel took the bottle out of his leather briefcase and said (as though announcing a birth): "Slivovitz. A Yugoslav liquor made from plums."

176

It's impossible to explain how the world suddenly paused. Bodily movements (the space-time of this act of love was the ocean) became a wink of fins. Aunt Magda, in slow motion, placed two crystal glasses on the table, and Pawel withdrew the cork from the bottle as though the corkscrew were a fiddler's bow.

177

Later they spoke (I recall) of Nefertiti. She was, without doubt, the fairest of women. She bore Amenhotep six daughters and after his death (fair as ever. Pawel had seen her portrait in a museum.) she married the son of a Hittite king (Shupiliuma) and shared her bed with Tutenkhamon.

178

Between the marble columns Nefertiti saw the face of Thoth, the god of the moon. Strange aromas arose from her body. But when she died, oxen lowed with dark pain along the canals and stone-cutters (fourteen hundred years before the birth of Christ) sang doleful songs.

179

After the war (in the winter of '74) God sent cold winds over the earth. In the clocks on the wall the alarm mechanisms (cuckoos and such like) froze. Aunt Magda kindled a blue

flame from her paraffin stove and they
sat (she and Frau Stier) on the old sofa,
side by side.

180

At five o'clock Frau Stier said "Ignatius." Did she mean the Bishop of
Antioch (Ignatius Theophoros) who
declared in his letters that a bishop
was worthy of the same respect as
God? Or did she mean Ignatius of
Loyola who (in St. Mary's Church. In
Montmartre.) founded the Order of
Jesuits? One way or the other, Frau
Stier said what she said and—as I live
and breathe!—if she were a character
in a novel (and not flesh and blood) she
would still be compelled (by some
other law) to say "Ignatius" at that
moment.

181

Spring came to the Northern Hemisphere only at the end of April. The rivers grew calm. The sea spewed forth wreckage. Waiters spread canvas sunshades and a thousand musicians blew (together. As in a Vivaldi concerto.) their flutes.

182

Cheesecakes flew, so great was the joy, on the wind. Forks soared to the clouds. Herr Doktor Staub leaned his chin on an imaginary marble slab and Hermina held between her fingers two kings. No doubt. It was an hour of grace. Thoughts took a back seat. Death was already present. But someone (it may have been Aunt Magda) said, "Frisch," and everyone played a second trump.

183

One day, when the great epic "Herr Doktor Staub in the Land of Israel" comes to be written, the tale will be told how Herr Doktor Staub took the bus to visit Hugo Jacobson, in Ramot Hashavim. What did Herr Doktor Staub want between the chicken runs? After all, Hugo Jacobson was dead. And even if he were not, had he not rejected (in 1936. In Braunschweig.) the opinion of Rudolf Carnap and Moritz Schlick that objects, per se, cannot be perceived?

184

In Kfar Saba, among the poplar trees, Herr Doktor Staub was already asking where the salt pits were. Hermina waved her hands in the air and laughed. And till they came to Hugo

Jacobson's house, the whole length of the way, hens (at first one after the other and finally in unison) could be heard proclaiming: "The salt pits are in Atlit, where Kurt and Ilse Lazarus live."

185

After lunch, Herr Doktor went to take a siesta. Gerda Jacobson (since the day Hugo died she had done everything alone) washed the dishes. But Hermina went for a walk outside on the red earth, and as she stood by the netting, little chicks made bold to come to her as though she were Mary, Mother of the Son of God.

186

In 1976 Aunt Magda had her teeth sharpened and on the stubs of the sharpened teeth they fitted porcelain crowns. The filaments of blood in her eyes ruptured. Her head drooped. She saw only the edges of things. From her eyeballs, around the iris which had muddied over, shone a dying light, as though from fragments of lakes.

187

She remembered Mancy Gross, who cried all night. No one could sleep, she cried so much.

188

She remembered her father, Isidore, standing in front of a button shop, his head almost touching the feet of Jesus, like some great bird. And when she came up to him, and he opened wide his coat, pearl buttons, she remembered (in the bands of light in Math-

iusch Square), rose from the boxes behind his back.

189

Apparently (even then. When her eyes
were failing.) she saw clear landscapes.
She said (to herself) *"Ich bin doch
Magda."* She listened to Memphis
Slim. But when Frau Stier rang the
doorbell she shouted *"Ich komm
schon"* and (just as she had in Pawel's
time. Once vertically and twice horizontally.) sliced the apple strudel.

190

Sometimes (at six o'clock in the
evening) Aunt Magda and Frau Stier
would go down to the beach, where the
Opera House once stood. They stuck
the tips of their canes between the

"But I am Magda" . . . *"I'm coming already"* (German)

cracked paving stones and froze against the rail like crocodiles. Their scaly tails stretched towards the falafel vendors and their Mesozoic eyes, hooded with skin, stared straight ahead.

191

What did their contemplation reveal? The beginning before which there is naught? The slight change, like an interruption? Desire? The body that takes shape, so very slowly, around the desire? The names? The things to which our desires give birth?

192

In Mograbi Square, under an enormous billboard, they bought ice cream. They knew very well that this outing was based in sin. It wasn't easy to ask for extra cherries. But as they carried their cones down Rechov Bograshov, past the display windows, they rose (both of them. Canes, dresses and all.) three cubits above the ground.

193

A pink bird tempts Mr. Moskowitz into thought. He thinks about swarms of bees. About soft armchairs. About the burial places of emperors. And when Casals said to Golda Myerson, "This is the cello that has accompanied me for half a century," Mr. Moskowitz cried.

Not because he loved music. He had never heard Casals in his life. He cried because Casals no longer drew his bow and the cello played by itself

and Casals said (he spoke very slowly):
"I love it and it loves me."

194

When Casals played his cello by
virtue of such love, he was ninety-six
years old. In the middle of Bach's C
Minor Suite, his dim eyes opened wide
and it was clear he was looking past
death at life. Mr. Moskowitz remembered those notes as though he himself
were the cello. His eyes surveyed his
inner organs. He heard the dead
breathing. From that day on all the
winds that blew were for Mr. Moskowitz internal winds.

It was a dreadful shock when his
hair began to grow inward, into his
body. This was the external sign of the
breakdown in the flow of time. His
hair returned, as it were, to that other

time that Casals had seen with blind eyes when he was ninety-six and playing Bach's Suite in C Minor, almost with no body.

From where Mr. Moskowitz was standing, the madness was crystal clear. His body was playing by itself, like Casals's cello. He was a resonating body nine hundred and sixty years old. There was no longer any need to do anything.

In sober moments his chin almost hit the floor. He ate so much from the other side of the mushroom. But when he grew tall a second time, he saw Romania as though it were entirely his own body as a child. Every single part of the mountainous organism. He was the sheep and the corn. He was the salted cheese.

All kinds of mirrors shattered, as though there had been a disaster in a glass warehouse. There were days when he sought himself at the end of the bed. He sat with his legs folded, between the springs, like a fakir. He *was* a fakir. When they asked (all the time) "Where is Mr. Moskowitz" they answered (others answered) "on his bed of nails."

195

No doubt of it. The nights of Palestine and Israel stretched like a roof over the heads of Aunt Magda and Frau Stier. Only the head of Mr. Moskowitz was exposed to the inverted abyss. He traveled with that caravan like a giraffe in a railway train. A skylight is breached and his head juts through. But the caravan, as the saying goes . . . and jackals (now very scarce) howl.

196

Herr Doktor Staub—loyal to the eternal law—changed his socks. His shirts were piled in the wardrobe like the skins of insects. He sloughed off one shirt and took on another. And it was bizarre. With all that abundance of colors, Herr Doktor Staub came in through the same entry (the Herr Doktor Staubian entry) all those years.

197

I remember lightning struck the tip of his walking stick. There was rain and a kind of orange light. Bright. Herr Doktor Staub was alarmed for a moment (you might call it "The Alarm Felt by Herr Doktor Staub on Seeing Sparks of Fire") and said, "There's electricity in the air."

198

How many philosophical theories were demolished in a flash of light! So the world does exist, and there are charges of electricity (and rays of light, refracted and diffracted, and glowing balls with sparkling tails, and necklaces of tiny pea-sized beads, and women with white necks standing like marzipan mushrooms in the air that is suddenly filled with electricity. On balconies.).

199

Two or three months after lightning struck the tip of his stick, Hermina died. One night, at about ten o'clock, she said, "I'm going to water the flowers" and walked straight out from the fourth floor. Sometimes, when winds blow through the rooms, you can see these elevated gardens: chrysanthemums spanning the road between the odd and even numbers, eight meters above the ground. She probably took a metal watering can and moved weightlessly through the curtains flapping in the wind, like the dancer said: "Floor? What's that?"

200

In years to come Herr Doktor Staub will say, "Her skin was almost transparent" and it will be strange to hear that in the end he was aware of transparency, even though he only saw her retrospectively, in thought. Then (when she went off the balcony, straight out into space) he still thought the laws of mechanics etcetera, etcetera.

201

How could one assume that Hermina's heavy body held a light spirit? In her frail body dwelt a heavy spirit that dragged her down and down by the hair of her head, while her body soared till it seemed a mere spark—a flash of aluminum—and was gone.

202

In 1977 Aunt Magda bought herself a pearl necklace. Scraps of sun danced on the counter and the jeweler as it were absentmindedly touched her hand. Some sights are unforgettable: her neck encircled by a pearl necklace on Ben Yehuda Street.

203

Her thoughts (above the little beads)
took her back, to Herbert and Theodor. You might almost say that the two
of them became a pearl Herbert-and-
Theodor. Secrets rose to the surface
like silhouettes of the Loch Ness
Monster: Herbert loved only her
brother Theodor, and married her
(i.e., Magda) for his sake. Theodor did
not love his wife. The two of them
(Laurel and Hardy, fat and thin) loved
only each other.

204

Suddenly she remembered (in her ring
of pearls) all manner of insults: how in
the heat of argument about the cate-
gories of Kant they failed to see that
she had prepared (all day it took her)

chicken paprika. How they brought in clods of mud and dirtied the floor. And she had asked them not to. How she had asked!

205

Her consciousness turned inwards upon itself, like a tailor who sews no clothes but his own. She and her sewing machine became a single entity. The cotton reels of memory spun tashibong tashibong. She sewed up herself.

206

She remembered Herbert's enormous belly by the light of the moon. In the adjoining room Theodor was sleeping and on the other side, at the end of the corridor, was the clinic. His belly should have covered the moon. Then she would have conceived. But he moved on the dark side of the room like a sad wrestler until the sun came out from hiding.

207

After they buried Hermina, Herr Doktor Staub thought: "Hermina is dead. What will I do now?" He saw a number of possibilities but not one of them was truly feasible. He could go back to Germany. He could enter an old age home, and he could fly.

208

The third was the most practical possibility. But he didn't know where to fit, to which bones of the back, the appropriate limbs. Furthermore, he thought, this option is only a temporary deferment of the other two. After all, he thought, when I take off the question will arise again in all its gravity: whither shall I fly? To Germany?

209

In addition, he was afraid of metal poisoning. The contact between iron wings and human flesh did not seem to Herr Doktor Staub sufficiently logical. If he had known at least that the device was one hundred percent reliable. But these days you can't be sure of anything. One way or another, he thought to himself, it would be as well to start with one cautious step (i.e., flight). A round-trip, for example, above North Tel Aviv as far as the outskirts of Herzlia and back.

210

He came to know great solitude.
Where once Hermina had been was
now a gaping hole, which went with
him like an absent hand or a missing
eye. The air he breathed was rarefied.
There was no one to balance the cosmic seesaw. His heavy intellect deaf-
ened him like an engine that malfunc-
tioned, and in the other direction he
saw only ugly, grim-visaged birds, as
though the sky housed some heavenly
academy and not clear air. Glass en-
compassing the world.

211

It's hard to picture him above the
chimneys of Reading Power Station,
his legs bent and the flaps of his winter
overcoat spread on the wind. What

would he not have given to bring back
Hermina's laugh? He suddenly under-
stood that Rudolf Carnap was dead
and his philosophical theory refuted,
for how was it conceivable that so
many transitory phenomena (like san-
dals and snails) could all together, like
an orchestra tuning up, fill the space of
the world with an out-of-tune A?
Anyway, this particular symphony, he
almost thought, had no need of well-
tempered notes.

212

In the third quarter of his year of
mourning, Herr Doktor Staub sat
himself down on Aunt Magda's old
sofa. His nasal septum bisected the air
but the praying mantis no longer re-
tained its sovereign powers. Frau Stier
sat opposite, by the harpsichord, and

when he turned to face her she
smoothed her silk dress over her knees
and gave a sigh.

213

When you think of Frau Stier you
must draw a picture that is both care-
ful and crude at one and the same time
(like a Chinese drawing. Not a line too
many.). This alone may perhaps be
said: before noon Frau Stier set the
dust flying in clouds and when the sun
began to set she looked at the crystal
chandelier in her room.

214

When Herr Stier died (a most awesome
occasion!), Frau Stier recalled, wine
was spilt. Frau Stier's wine and the
wines (Bordeaux, port, Madeira, etc.)

in the wine store. Now (the same miracle) the wine turned into water and the
water into air and the air into memory.

215

Things not to be spoken of occurred in
those days, as when someone slammed
the shop door and stood in front of
rows of bottles. No painter (except the
divine Portraitist) could paint such a
picture: the elixir imprisoned in glass
cylinders and people helping themselves again and again.

216

In 1978 Aunt Magda saw ships on Rechov Dizengoff. She thrust her walking stick in front of her towards a large
store dealing in curtains, and said:
"Schau! Ein Schiff!"

"Look! A ship!" (German)

217

From certain points of view the curtain store was indeed afloat. Women named Camellia leaned their bodies against the display windows. They uttered incomparably beautiful things and the sailing vessel sailed away (Lights. Glass.) to streets of a different realm. More pellucid.

218

You need imagination to picture Aunt Magda at the bus station. In January. How can one know the concrete reality of things? Even when everything has been said, the dreadful residue remains: her toes in their shoes. Five in each (together with Frau Stier's feet—two times ten).

219

In February Herr Doktor Staub went to visit Gerda Jacobson. Gerda Jacobson was sitting in the sun. On the verandah. And though between the tiny particles of her body (electrons, etc.) there was space, you could not see through her.

220

That day Herr Doktor Staub heard bird songs. He could tell Bachbirds from Mahlerbirds. The ears he had brought with him from Braunschweig revolved like saucer antennae:

Tweetweetweet.

Tweetweetwah.

Tweetweetweetweetweetweetweet.

Tweetweetweetweetweetweetwah.

And again tweetweetweet.

And again tweetweetwah.

And once more tweetweetweet-weetweet.

And once more tweetweetweet-weetwah.

221

In days to come, when Herr Doktor Staub thought of Eastern Palestine, he pictured in his mind the house of Hugo Jacobson. First of all—Hugo's brain hemorrhage. Then—sitting in the sun—Gerda with matzo crumbs on her chin.

222

In March Aunt Magda heard the oom-pah-oompah of the waterpipes.

223

She was lying down. In bed. In extremis. Something wrong with her legs. The gods of war urged her to put on her pearls. But she turned her head aside and like Mancy Gross, who wore glasses (everything seemed to Mancy Gross bigger than it was) she cried.

224

Frau Stier placed a carton of buttermilk on the night table. Herr Doktor Staub carried flowers (I remember) up the stairs. It's hard to keep people on the Earth's crust. Nevertheless. In

April she—Aunt Magda—regained her power of rummy and her power of apple strudel.

225

The Land of Israel lay open before Herr Doktor Staub. He journeyed to the Dead Sea and the Great Wilderness. Warm breezes caressed his head. He saw gazelles. Hills from the Cenozoic Era passed before him.

226

He remembered (at the base of the Rift Valley. Between the salt rocks.) the University of Heidelberg.

227

Things of no moment (like the way a Bedouin child ran) broke his heart.

228

To the north of his body lay the world
to the north of his body. To the south
of his body—the world to his south.
Kings of Moab stood on the peaks opposite, and way above (the dogs of his
childhood came back to him. The
schnauzer and the Labrador bitch.) lay
the sun and the moon and the stars.

229

In May (there was a *khamsin*, I remember) Aunt Magda said, "I can't
see." Total blackness had suddenly de-
scended upon her vision, and it was
clear from the sound of her voice that
the world she had known, where the
kettle appeared as a thin metal band,
was infinitely preferable.

230

She was terrified. Her head and the two marbles in it sought the splash of reflected light.

231

If only she could have seen the light separate from the things. In huge containers. She could have split it into colors by herself. She appealed to Herbert by name

232

(and one could see how she moved before the War).

233

And through the power of that appeal
(from out of her blindness. Two or
three weeks before she died.) she saw a
great vision and everything was in it.
She saw the soul of the carp. And the
soul of the birds. And the soul of her
brooches. And of her porcelain cups.
And of her iron. And her purse. And
the soul of the ginger, the vanilla, and
the playing cards. And she knew (oh,
yes, she knew!) that this world continues into the next unchanged. There is
no division. Only the directions are
reversed.